nickelodeon

# DORA the EXPLORER

# HALLOWEEN Hoedown!

By Molly Reisner

Illustrated by Dave Aikins

A Random House PICTUREBACK® Book

Random House 🏠 New York

ISBN 978-0-449-81762-9
randomhouse.com/kids
Printed in the United States of America
10 9 8 7 6 5 4 3 2 1

Dora and Boots were getting ready to celebrate Halloween. Their friend Benny was having a costume dance party at his barn. He was calling the party the Halloween Hoedown!

"I'm a tiger! *¡Un tigre!*" roared Dora as she zipped up her furry costume.

"And I'm going to be a clown," said Boots. "I'm going to make everyone at the hoedown laugh with my silly clown dance!" He juggled his pointy hat, his red nose, and his big blue clown shoes.

"That's so funny, Boots!" giggled Dora. "But you'd better put on your costume now! Benny's Halloween Hoedown is starting soon!"

Just then, a jack-o'-lantern rolled out of the bushes toward Dora and Boots. But it wasn't just a jack-o'-lantern— it was Swiper! The sneaky fox grabbed Boots's clown costume and tossed it far away. "Heh-heh-heh! You'll never find it now!" said Swiper, and he rolled off.

"Oh, no! My costume! I need it for the Halloween Hoedown!" cried Boots.

Dora hugged Boots. "Don't worry. We'll find it before the hoedown starts," she promised her friend.

"Who do we ask for help when we don't know which way to go?" asked Dora.

"Map!" answered Boots.

Map hopped right out of Backpack. He was wearing a pirate costume!

"Ahoy, mateys!" said Map. "To get your costume back, just listen to me—your Treasure Map! You'll find the pointy hat in the Haunted Garden. You'll find the red nose in the Spooky Forest. And the big blue shoes are on the roof of the barn at Benny's Halloween Hoedown!"

Dora and Boots set out for the Haunted Garden, but suddenly, the path split in two!

Dora saw a post with two signs hanging on it. One had a picture of a spooky garden, and the other had a picture of a spooky house.

"Look! This sign says the Haunted Garden is on the path with the purple bats. Come on, Boots!" said Dora.

At the Haunted Garden, Dora and Boots met a ghost with a green tail. "We don't know any ghosts," Dora said, giggling, "but do we know someone with a green tail?"

"Isa!" Boots shouted.

"We need to find Boots's pointy hat," said Dora.

"I'll help you look for it," said Isa.

Together, they searched in a pumpkin patch. Isa had decorated it with silly ghosts, all wearing hats. But one ghost had something else on his head. . . .

"My hat!" Boots cheered.

Isa put the pointy hat on Boots's head.

"Thanks for helping, Isa," said Boots, smiling. "See you at the party!"

Next, Dora and Boots raced to the Spooky Forest to find the red nose. "This place sure is spooky," said Boots, looking around. "And spiky, too! Dora, how are we going to get past these spiky plants?"

Dora pointed to a row of colorful vines that hung from the trees. "We need to swing from vine to vine to get past them!"

Dora and Boots grabbed the closest vine and started to swing over the spiky plants.

"Let's name the colors as we go!" Dora cheered.

"¡Amarillo! Yellow! ¡Rosado! Pink! ¡Azul! Blue! ¡Verde! Green! ¡Rojo! Red! ¡Morado! Purple!" they called out together.

After jumping off the purple vine, Dora and Boots landed next to some decorated jack-o'-lanterns. Each one had a different nose!

"Does one of them have your red nose, Boots?" Dora asked.

Boots spotted the red nose, ran over, and plucked it from the pumpkin.

"My nose!" He smiled and placed it on his face.

"*¡Vámonos!* Let's hurry to Benny's barn so we can find your shoes before the Halloween Hoedown starts!" said Dora.

Suddenly, Dora and Boots heard a honk. It was their friend Tico in an astronaut suit. He was driving a spaceship car! Tico offered Dora and Boots a ride to the party.

But a thick layer of fog lay over the road. "It's too foggy for Tico to drive!" said Boots.

Dora noticed some twinkling lights in the trees. "I see some friends who can help us—the Bugga Bugga Bugs! If we call to them, they can light the way! On the count of three, let's yell 'Bugga Buggas!' *¡Uno! ¡Dos! ¡Tres!*"

"Bugga Buggas!" the three friends shouted.

Mama Bugga Bugga and her babies buzzed over to Dora, Boots, and Tico, their bright taillights glowing. Tico could see the road again! He followed the Bugga Buggas all the way to the Halloween Hoedown.

"*Gracias*, Tico," Dora said as she and Boots hopped out of the car.

Outside Benny's Barn, music was playing. The party was
about to begin. But Boots still needed to find his big blue shoes!
He jumped up and down, pointing at the roof of the barn.
"My shoes! There they are!" he said. "But how will we get all
the way up there?"

Big Red Chicken, who was dressed as a big red witch, had an idea. "I brought my magic broom to the party. You can use it to fly up and get your shoes! You just have to say the magic words. 'Broom, broom, you can fly! Give us a lift into the sky!'"

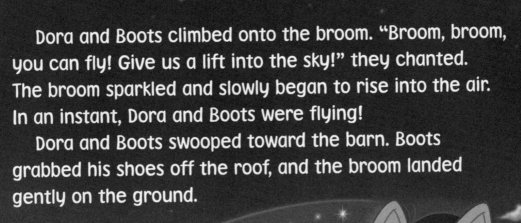

Dora and Boots climbed onto the broom. "Broom, broom, you can fly! Give us a lift into the sky!" they chanted. The broom sparkled and slowly began to rise into the air. In an instant, Dora and Boots were flying!

Dora and Boots swooped toward the barn. Boots grabbed his shoes off the roof, and the broom landed gently on the ground.

Boots put on his big blue shoes. His clown costume was complete!
"We did it!" cheered Dora.

Inside the barn, everyone was dressed up for Halloween. "Time to start the Halloween Hoedown! Grab a partner!" said Benny. The Fiesta Trio played a fast song. Dora and Boots linked arms and spun in a circle.

"And now for a special treat. Boots the Clown will do his special clown dance!" announced Benny.

Boots stood in the center of the room and did his funny clown dance. The crowd laughed and cheered and danced around him.

"Happy Halloween, everybody!" said Dora.